21st
Century
Skills Library

GLOBAL PRODUCTS

ATHLETIC SHOES

Dana Meachen Rau

Cherry Lake Publishing
Ann Arbor, Michigan

Published in the United States of America by Cherry Lake Publishing
Ann Arbor, MI
www.cherrylakepublishing.com

Content Adviser: Cameron Kippen, Podologist and Sneaker Historian, Lecturer at
Charles Sturt University, Albury, New South Wales, Australia

Photo Credits: Cover and page 1, © Gareth Brown/Corbis; page 7, © Bobby Yip/Reuters/
Corbis; page 8, © Steve Raymer/Corbis; page 15, © Dean Conger/Corbis; page 16, ©
Mike Cassese/Reuters/Corbis; page 23, © Richard Clement/Reuters/Corbis; page 24, ©
Steve Raymer/Corbis

Map by XNR Productions Inc.

Library of Congress Cataloging-in-Publication Data
Rau, Dana Meachen, 1971–
  Athletic shoes / by Dana Meachen Rau.
    p. cm. — (Global products)
  ISBN-13: 978-1-60279-027-8 (hardcover)
  ISBN-10: 1-60279-027-2 (hardcover)
  1. Athletic shoes—Juvenile literature. 2. Athletic shoes—History—Juvenile literature.
I. Title. II. Series.
  GV749.S64R38 2007
  685.36—dc22   2007003886

Cherry Lake Publishing would like to acknowledge the work of
The Partnership for 21st Century Skills.
Please visit www.21stcenturyskills.org *for more information.*

TABLE OF CONTENTS

CHAPTER ONE

FROM PLIMSOLLS
TO COMPUTER CHIPS

*Runners and other athletes depend on athletic
shoes to help them compete.*

Zoe's heart was beating hard. She couldn't wait for the race to get started.
Kelly was ready, too, her number pinned to her shirt.

"Nice shoes," Zoe said. Usually, girls from competing schools didn't talk
to each other before a race. But Zoe noticed that Kelly had the same sleek,
light athletic shoes as she did.

"Just got them," Kelly said. "They make me feel like I'm running on air."

"You are," Zoe said. "Those are the kind of shoes with pockets of air in the soles."

"Imagine what the ancient Greeks must have felt," Kelly said. "They ran marathons barefoot!"

"Well, at least this isn't a marathon," Zoe said. "Just three miles."

"And at least we have good shoes!" Kelly laughed.

They heard the coach say, "Runners set!" Next came the blast of the starting pistol.

Zoe and Kelly were off and running, along with the rest of their cross-country teammates. Through the bumpy trails, the girls could hardly feel the roots and rocks under their well-cushioned shoes.

Athletes of all sports—including running, basketball, tennis, and soccer—wear athletic shoes. Even if you are not a professional athlete, you probably wear them, too. Whether you play sports after school, in physical education class, or just go for a walk with friends, athletic shoes are always a reliable choice for footwear. Each year in the United States, people buy about 350 million pairs of athletic shoes.

What Zoe and Kelly probably don't know is how athletic shoes have evolved over the years to allow both of them to soar through their cross-country meets effortlessly.

The history of athletic shoes as we know them today starts in the 1800s. A new method of processing rubber, called **vulcanization**, made rubber soft and bendy. People thought it might be a good material for the soles of shoes. Rubber-soled shoes called plimsolls were some of the earliest shoes for sports, although they had no right or left foot. In the late 1800s, the U.S. Rubber Company made shoes with a rubber sole and a canvas top that were more comfortable. By 1917, they started mass-producing their sports shoes called Keds.

Many American athletic shoe companies began after that. They started making shoes specific to sports such as basketball, tennis, and baseball, which were becoming more popular early in the 1900s. Then athletic shoes went global. In 1924, Adi Dassler started up his company, Adidas, in Germany, and Germans led the athletic shoe industry.

Athletic shoes were in more demand in the middle of the century. In the 1950s, people started dressing more comfortably, and kids started wearing more athletic shoes. In the 1960s, the need for shoes for sports played a big role in the growth of the athletic shoe industry.

Athletic shoe sales soared as athletes started to **endorse** shoes. In the 1980s, Michael Jordan's famous Air Jordans brought sales to a new level. Specialized athletic shoes started to be produced for all kinds of sports.

Many athletic shoe companies shifted their production overseas, where Asian countries had newly opened to world trade. Fewer shoes were made in the United States. Many Asian countries, such as South Korea

Michael Jordan speaks at a news conference in Hong Kong during his promotional tour for Nike in 2004.

and Taiwan, had updated technologies that could keep up with fast-paced changes in the shoe industry. Companies also moved production overseas because labor was cheaper there. In poorer countries, such as China or Thailand, workers were willing to accept much lower wages than workers in the United States.

Today's athletic shoes have some amazing features. The Nike+ running shoe has a computer chip that can communicate with your MP3 player

Workers assemble athletic shoes in a factory in Vietnam.

so that it can tell you how far you have run while it plays songs to keep you going. Other shoes are so cushioned that you feel like you are running on air.

Zoe raced up next to Kelly. "How are your feet feeling?" asked Zoe.

"Awesome!" replied Kelly as she took a deep breath. "It feels like I'm not even running on the ground!"

"Too bad they can't push me up this hill!" Zoe laughed.

The girls went their separate ways for the remainder of the race, but both began to wonder how these shoes could take so much punishment from the ground below and still remain so comfortable.

Why do you think some people call athletic shoes "sneakers"? Athletic shoes are sometimes called sneakers because the use of rubber for soles made the shoes quiet, so you could easily sneak up on someone. In fact, before the late 1960s, many people associated this type of footwear with criminal behavior because thieves could move around quietly in sneakers to lessen the risk of being caught. What are some of the factors that changed this perception of sneakers and made wearing them more acceptable by the late 1960s?

CHAPTER TWO

WHERE THE SHOE HITS THE ROAD

The upper is the part of the shoes that covers most of your foot. The bottom of the shoe is called the outsole.

Athletes around the world wear athletic shoes, just like Zoe and Kelly. But few runners know exactly how athletic shoes are produced or what they are made out of. But these can be important factors to consider when selecting an athletic shoe to fit your needs.

Athletic shoes can be made of up to 20 different components, or parts. Let's take a "tour" of a typical athletic shoe to see some of its basic parts.

The **upper** is the top part of the shoe made of **synthetic** leather, nylon mesh, canvas, or other materials. Nylon mesh is especially helpful for runners like Zoe and Kelly. It allows feet to "breathe" a bit inside of the shoe when they run long distances. The upper of an athletic shoe also includes the laces, tongue, and the logo and any designs the company places on the shoe.

The **outsole** is the bottom of the shoe that hits the ground. It is covered by bumps and treads to give you traction, or a better grip, on the ground. Shoes with good traction provide better stability for people who run in cross-country meets over bumpy terrain. Outsoles are usually made of synthetic rubber. They may also be made of natural rubber or a mixture of both.

The **midsole** is one of the most important parts of an athletic shoe. It cushions and supports your feet to make your shoes feel comfortable and bouncy. Midsoles are made of man-made foam materials, such as **polyurethane** or **EVA** (ethylene vinyl acetate). In the heel, or wedge, the midsole might surround a tough plastic capsule of air or gel to give extra support. A great midsole is the reason why Zoe and Kelly feel like they are running on air. It provides their feet with support.

The rubber for the outsoles in not processed in the same factory where the shoes are put together. Natural rubber is harvested on rubber plantations in Thailand, Indonesia, China, or other tropical places where

Latex oozes out of a rubber tree.

Hevea rubber trees grow best. A metal spout is inserted into the bark of a tree. A white sap, called latex, oozes out. The latex is combined in a tank where the water is removed. The rubber left behind is made into crumbs or sheets, and baled up to be shipped to athletic shoe manufacturers.

Synthetic rubber is made by companies in countries around the globe, including Germany, China, Russia, and Japan. Synthetic rubber is made from chemicals derived by processing **petroleum**. These chemicals might be made right at the plant or arrive in tank trucks. The chemicals are mixed together in tanks and heated or cooled. The rubber that results is then ready to be shipped.

For the midsole, polyurethane is made from mixing chemicals and gases and heating them in a certain way to react to each other and create a foam substance. EVA is also made by mixing chemicals and gases together. The polyurethane or EVA foam is made into thick plates that can then be heated and molded into their desired shapes at the manufacturer.

CHAPTER THREE

Melting and Molding

So what goes into the manufacturing of athletic shoes like Zoe's and Kelly's? Among many other steps, it involves a highly complex process of melting and molding to create the athletic shoe's parts that keep people stable, bouncy, and comfortable. Everything from the rubber soles to the nylon/mesh uppers are gathered by manufacturers from all over the world and are produced in factories in different countries.

Bales and rolls of rubber and other materials are transported by truck or plane to a factory. The method of transportation used depends on how far the materials have to be shipped. But even when the rubber and foam arrive at the shoe manufacturer's facility, they still have a long way to go before they become shoes. They need to be made into the outsoles and midsoles.

For outsoles, workers cut thick strips of rubber down to the size needed for the bottom of the shoe and place it on a mold. Then the rubber is compressed and heated at the same time so that as it melts, it takes the form of the mold. This is called compression molding. This also vulcanizes the rubber.

Some outsoles also have blown rubber. The blowing process makes the rubber spongier. Some of the chemicals in the rubber turn to gas when

Bales of rubber are loaded onto a barge in Thailand.

they are heated and create bubbles of air that make the rubber softer and lighter.

The midsole may also be made using compression molding. If EVA is used for the midsole, the foam is cut, placed on a mold, and

21st Century Content

Many companies look for ways to recycle materials. They do this in an attempt to save money or in response to customers who want to do business with companies whose manufacturing methods don't harm the environment. Over the past decade, millions of athletic shoes have been collected and ground down to create a material that can be used to make running tracks and other play surfaces. Nike's Reuse-A-Shoe program makes the shoes into a material they call Nike Grind. They also use this material, mixed with others, to create injection-molded midsoles for new shoes.

Canadian football player Damon Allen looks at a model of a stadium that will be built using the recycled athletic shoe material known as Nike Grind.

compressed and heated into the proper shape. Sometimes pellets of EVA are used. The right amount of pellets are weighed, placed into a mold, and heated until they melt into the midsole shape. Midsoles can also be made by injecting the material into a mold. This is called **injection molding**.

All materials used for outsoles and midsoles have their advantages and disadvantages. For the outsole, carbon rubber is the most durable, but blown rubber is lighter and bouncier. In the midsole, polyurethane is the most durable but is heavier than EVA. However, EVA, while light, can lose its bounciness quicker.

Some athletic shoe companies, such as Brooks Running, have tried mixing rubber materials and EVA into one sole—the outsole and insole are one piece. Rubber and EVA cannot be mixed by compression molding because the temperatures needed are different for the two materials. But they can be injection molded together. This makes the shoe much lighter, which pleases runners who need to be fast.

Learning & Innovation Skills

Ideas for new types of shoes come from studying how people play and how their bodies work. But some ideas have come from space. Blown rubber was first used to make lightweight helmets for astronauts. NASA engineer Frank Rudy took the idea to Nike, which wound up creating Nike Air, a cushioning system in the midsole.

CHAPTER FOUR

Making Them Last

Zoe and Kelly race in many cross-country meets each year. They run over all different types of terrain and up and down hills. So how do their shoes manage not to get torn up, worn out, or destroyed? How do the rubber soles manage to stay strong for so long and after so much stress? The answer lies in the production of the shoe itself. Manufacturers put lots of effort into making sure their shoes are safe, reliable, and will go the distance.

Some components of an athletic shoe, such as the outsoles or midsoles, may be made in one factory and then brought to another factory, where all the pieces of the shoe are put together. Hundreds of workers and machines are involved in the process. Machines may do much of the work that was once done by people, but the machines still need human operators. There may be more than 100 people working on an assembly line in an athletic shoe factory.

On an assembly line, one person is in charge of a certain task, such as stitching certain pieces together or operating a particular machine. The shoes might travel along a conveyor belt that brings the shoes from station to station, depending on what work needs to be done.

*Some athletic shoes are designed
for people who play tennis.*

Teams of researchers, scientists, and doctors often help design new shoes. The ASICS Research Institute of Sports Science in Kobe, Japan, is a 45,000-plus-square-foot (4,180-plus-square-meter) research facility. It contains everything needed to create the next best shoe. It has many sports surfaces, such as tracks, courts, and fields. It has computers to analyze how the body moves. And it has labs to test the strength and durability of different materials.

The upper is made from material delivered to the factory in large rolls. A **die-cutting machine** cuts out all the shapes needed for the upper like a big cookie cutter. These pieces are brought to another part of the factory.

There the upper pieces are stitched together. At some factories, workers do this by hand on sewing machines. Other athletic shoe companies use computer-controlled stitching machines. After the upper pieces are stitched together, an **insole**, which supports the arch of your foot, is stitched to the upper. Now the piece looks like a shoe without the thick bottom.

One of the most important tools of the next part of the assembly process is the **last**. A last looks like a foot and is made of plastic, wood, or metal. A machine or worker stretches the shoe over the last. The last helps give the shoe its shape. There are different lasts for different shoe sizes, as well as different ones for left and right shoes and for men and women.

Lasts are shaped like feet and used in the production of all kinds of shoes.

Meanwhile, the midsole and outsole have been cemented together. While the shoe is on the last, a **roughing robot** or a worker makes the bottom of the shoe rough so that the glue will stick better. Then it moves to a station where someone cements the midsole and outsole to the bottom of the shoe.

At the end of the assembly line, an inspector checks each shoe to be sure all of the components have been assembled perfectly. Workers then

Factory workers aren't the only workers involved in getting athletic shoes into the hands of customers. Other workers from around the world play a part. Executives run the company. Truck drivers and ship crews transport the shoes. Dockworkers unload them. Clerks at stores sell them to customers. All of these people need to be able to work together when necessary. This often means understanding the culture and customs of another country so you can interact appropriately with colleagues from that country.

lace the shoes partway, wrap them in tissue paper, and place them in labeled shoe boxes. All of these boxes are placed in larger boxes and are ready to be transported.

The boxes of shoes are loaded into large containers provided by the shipping company. Trucks bring these containers to the port, where large cranes load them onto a cargo ship. Shoes may not be the only product that a ship will carry. The warehouse-like space on the cargo ship may also have containers of toys, computers, or other products.

When the ship reaches the United States, the containers wait at the port for trucks to pick them up. The trucks bring them to warehouses. Orders for stores are filled from the warehouses, and other trucks will deliver the orders to stores, where clerks unload the shoe boxes and display the shoes on their shelves for you to buy.

CHAPTER FIVE

SOMEONE ELSE'S SHOES

*You can find many different brands and styles
of athletic shoes in shoe stores.*

When Zoe and Kelly bought their running shoes, they probably considered a few things before making the purchase. They may have been looking for a particular color, style, or brand name.

A worker walks past an athletic shoe factory building in Vietnam.

Regardless of what factors people consider when they shop for athletic shoes, it is likely that few, if any, of them stop to consider the individuals who made the shoes in the factory. The fact remains that many of the people who put together the shoes in factories are from many different parts of the globe. Whether it's Taiwan, China, Japan, Indonesia, or Mexico, workers from all over the world have a hand in putting together your athletic shoes.

Have you ever heard the expression "to walk in someone else's shoes?" It means you should think about what it is like to be someone else and what they might experience that is different than you. What do you think it is like to walk in the shoes of a factory worker in China? Or the captain of a cargo ship? Or a trucker delivering shoes to a local store? Many people from many countries are part of the process that puts shoes on your feet so that you can walk in them.

Globalization means that companies in many countries are involved in the making of a product. World trade has been alive throughout history, but it once meant that one country traded finished products with another. A global economy today means that one country might produce the raw materials, another country might make a component, and yet another might manufacture those components into a finished product. Then those finished products might be exported to many countries, to be sold to customers.

Nike, Reebok, and Adidas (which now owns Reebok) are major athletic shoe manufacturers that **import** 100 percent of their shoes from Asia, mostly from China. ASICS is an athletic shoe company based in Japan. New Balance is the only major manufacturer of athletic shoes in the United States, although they also import some components from Asia.

Learning & Innovation Skills

How do people who start companies come up with names for their companies? It takes a lot of creative thinking to come up with just the right name. Here are a few examples:

- Nike: named after the Greek goddess of victory
- Reebok: named after a type of African gazelle
- Adidas: named for its founder—Adi (Adolf) Dassler
- ASICS: the first letters of the words in the Latin phrase *anima sana in corpore sano*, which means "a sound mind in a sound body"

  If you started an athletic shoe company, what would you name it?

People all over the world wear athletic shoes while playing soccer and other sports. These students are in Tunisia.

Most of the large athletic shoe companies are multinational corporations. This means that even though the assembly of shoes might be done mostly in Asia, the companies also have offices around the world on almost every continent.

Your athletic shoes have traveled a long road before you ever lace them up. You might be wearing them for the first time to school or a park or a game, but they likely have already journeyed halfway around the world.

~

When the race was over, and Zoe and Kelly met at the finish line, they were both exhausted.

"Wow! That was some race, wasn't it?" Kelly asked as they walked together, trying to catch their breath.

"Yeah, tough," Zoe replied. "At least my feet didn't blister up."

Kelly pointed to her feet. "Mine either," she said. "These are great shoes."

"Can't wait to use them again next time," Zoe said.

"I'll be there!" Kelly smiled. "And my shoes and I will be faster than ever!"

21st Century Content

The World Trade Organization (WTO) aims at making it easier for countries to share their goods. Other agreements, such as the North American Free Trade Agreement (NAFTA), have also made trade easier around the globe.

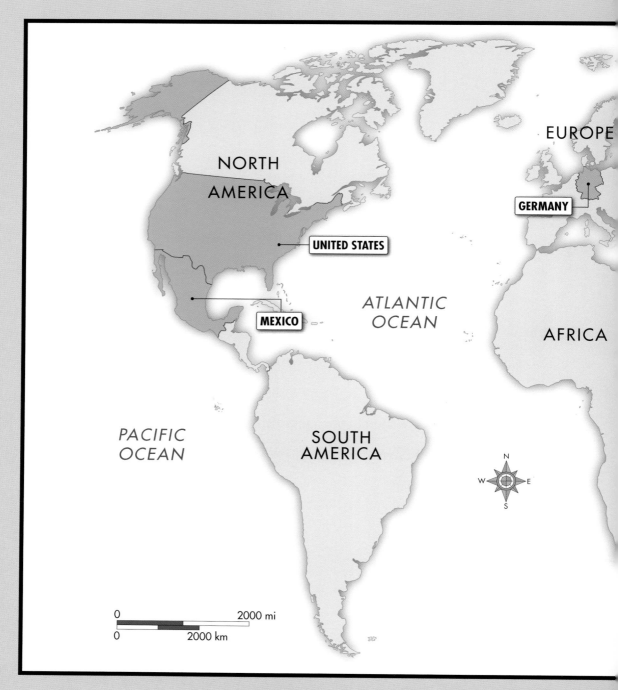

NORTH
AMERICA

GERMANY

EUROPE

UNITED STATES

MEXICO

ATLANTIC
OCEAN

AFRICA

PACIFIC
OCEAN

SOUTH
AMERICA

N
W   E
S

0   2000 mi
0   2000 km

This map shows the countries and cities mentioned in the text.

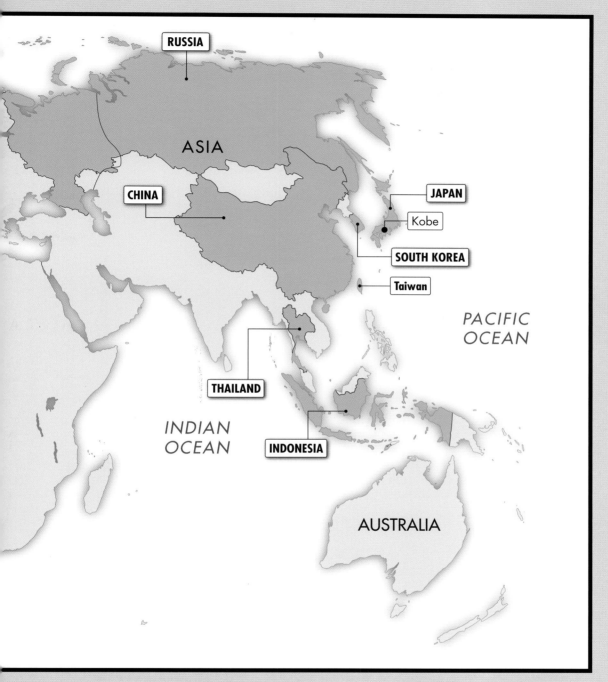

They are the locations of some of the companies involved in the making and selling of athletic shoes.

GLOSSARY

die-cutting machine (DYE KUT-ing muh-SHEEN) a machine that cuts out all the shapes needed to manufacture something, such as the upper of a shoe

endorse (en-DORS) to use one's fame to help sell a product

EVA (EE-VEE-AY) ethylene vinyl acetate; a man-made foamy material used in making athletic shoe midsoles

exporting (eks-PORT-ing) sending goods out of one country to be sold in another country

import (IM-port) to bring goods into one country from another country

insole (IN-sole) the part of the shoe between the bottom of your foot and the midsole

midsole (MID-sole) the part of the shoe that provides cushioning for your foot

outsole (OUT-sole) the bottom of the shoe that touches the ground

petroleum (puh-TRO-lee-um) an oily liquid used to make gasoline and other products

polyurethane (pah-lee-YUR-uh-thane) a man-made foamy material used for making athletic shoe midsoles and other products

roughing robot (RUFF-ing RO-bot) a machine that rubs the bottom of an insole to make the surface better able to hold glue

synthetic (sin-THEH-tik) artificial; made by humans

upper (UP-er) the top part of an athletic shoe that covers the top and sides of your foot

vulcanization (vul-kun-ih-ZAY-shun) the process of heating rubber so that it stays strong and pliable in all temperatures and doesn't get sticky when it is too hot or crack when it is too cold

FOR MORE INFORMATION

Books

Bookbinder, Stephen, and Lynne Einleger. *The Dictionary of the Global Economy*. Danbury, CT: Franklin Watts, 2001.

Cobb, Vicki. *Sneakers*. Minneapolis: Millbrook Press, 2006.

Web Sites

Nike Reuse-A-Shoe Program
www.nikereuseashoe.com
Information about Nike's athletic shoe recycling program

American Academy of Orthopaedic Surgeons: Athletic Shoes
orthoinfo.aaos.org/fact/thr_report.cfm?thread_id=32
For information on getting the proper fit when purchasing new athletic shoes

INDEX

ABOUT THE AUTHOR

Dana Meachen Rau is the author of more than 200 books for children. She has written a variety of nonfiction titles on many subjects, including books on history, science, toys, and crafts, as well as biographies. When she is not working in her home office, she is outside walking or running in her sneakers around her neighborhood in Burlington, Connecticut.